The Berenstain Bears
and
TOO MUCH TV

When the TV is on
All day without rest,
Mama knows it's too much—
And Mama knows best.

A FIRST TIME BOOK®

SUMMARY: Concerned that the family is spending too much time in front of the television and neglecting other activities, Mama Bear decides that there will be no television watching for one week. [1. Television—Fiction. 2. Bears—Fiction] I. Berenstain, Jan. II. Title. III. Series. PZ7.B4483Bem 1984 [E] 83-22887 ISBN: 0-394-86570-7 (trade); 0-394-96570-1 (lib. bdg.) Manufactured in the United States of America

The Berenstain Bears and
and
TOO MUCH TV

Stan & Jan Berenstain

Random House 🏠 New York

It was a fine spring day in Bear Country. The bluebirds were singing. The trout were leaping. And except for one small cloud of dust billowing behind the school bus as it came over the hill, the air was sparkling clean.

Mama Bear was inside the family's tree house fixing Brother and Sister Bear's after-school snack.

Brother and Sister Bear got off the school bus
and came into the kitchen with hardly a hello.
Then they did what they did every day: They took
their milk and cookies into the living room and
switched on the TV.

"There's no question about it," thought Mama.
"Those cubs are watching too much TV!"

Later, when Papa Bear came in from his shop and joined Brother and Sister, Mama became even more convinced....

"There's absolutely no question about it. The whole Bear family is watching too much TV!"

She wasn't quite sure
how it had happened. Maybe
it began when the old
fuzzy-pictured black and
white set broke down and
they got a big new color set.

Or maybe it started when Papa put the big antenna up on top of the tree house and brought in pictures from all over Bear Country.

But however it had happened, one thing was sure—the Bear family was spending more and more time watching television and less and less time with all the other things they might be doing instead.

The Bear family had always had lively conversations around the dinner table—

—but not lately. Lately they just sat around and chewed.

The cubs had all kinds of fun playing outdoors. But not anymore.

They were too busy watching *Nutty Bear* and *The Bear Stooges*.

That evening after dinner, when
Brother and Sister scampered in to turn
on the TV, Mama stopped them and said
her piece: "We've been watching altogether
too much television around here!"

"But, Mama," said Brother. "*Nutty Bear*
is coming on and we'll miss it!"

"And *The Bear Stooges*!" added Sister.

"Well, you'll just have to miss them!" said
Mama firmly.

"And furthermore," she added, "you may as well get used to the idea because there's *not going to be any television around here for a whole week!*"

"No TV for a week!?" said the shocked cubs. "But, Mama..."

"Never mind the *buts*," said Papa. "Your mother
is absolutely right. There's a lot more to life
than TV—like homework, for instance. And fresh
air and sunshine. And exercise. No TV for a week
is an excellent idea....

   "Now, if you'll excuse me, there's a sports show
I want to watch."

"Just a moment, Papa," said Mama. "No TV for a week means you, too."

"What?!" said Papa. "You can't be serious!"

But Mama was very serious.

"What about the news?" protested Papa. "I won't know what's going on in the world if I don't watch the TV news!"

"Here, try this," said Mama. "It's called the newspaper."

"And the weather!" continued Papa. "How will we know what the weather will be?"

"Try this," said Mama. "It's called putting your hand out the window to see if it's raining."

"What are we supposed to do—just sit around and talk?" asked Brother.

"That'll be fine for starters," said Mama, settling comfortably into her rocker.

But it had been so long since the Bear family sat around and talked that they had sort of forgotten how.

It really didn't matter, because pretty soon Papa fell asleep and snored so loudly that they wouldn't have heard each other anyway.

After school the next day, the cubs looked longingly at the TV but Mama shooed them out to play.

Brother's bike had a tire that needed pumping up and Sister's trike needed a little oil—and while it seemed strange not watching television, it was fun riding bikes and trikes again. Sort of.

That evening the cubs worked on their homework. But it wasn't easy with that blank TV just sitting there staring.

Then Sister noticed an ad in Papa's newspaper—an ad for a TV special.

"Oh, Mama!" she said. "Look! A special!"

"No TV for a week means no TV for a week," answered Mama. "And besides, Mother Nature has a much bigger special waiting for us. We're going to sit outside and watch the stars come out."

"Watch the stars come out?!" complained Sister.

"I don't know if I can stand the excitement," said Brother.

But as they sat out under the great sky, a spell came over the bears. It was all so big and beautiful. The bears stared at the sky. So far, not a single star.

"Look!" cried Sister. "Something flying!"

"Bats," said Papa. "Out for their breakfast of insects."

"Breakfast?" asked Brother.

"That's right," answered Papa. "Bats sleep during the day, so this is their breakfast time."

"I see a star!" cried Sister. She had found the first tiny star.

Soon there were others.

And after a while the whole sky was full of stars.

And it was very special—more special than anything they'd ever seen on TV. It was a sharper picture, too—and a much, much, *much* bigger screen.

The Bear family did all sorts of interesting things over the next few days—so interesting that they hardly thought about TV.

They went on a nature walk and watched tadpoles hatch out of eggs.

They watched an orb spider spin a magnificent web.

They went shopping at the Bear
Country Mall. Sister used some of
her savings to buy a knitting spool
and some yarn. Brother bought a
cube puzzle.

They did have to keep an eye on
Papa, though.

When they were at the mall, the cubs caught Papa in the TV store sneaking a look at a game show.

Another time he went downstairs in the middle of the night for a peek at the late-late movie, but Mama and the cubs stopped him just in time.

The next evening—it was the last day of their no-TV week—the Bear family was having a lively conversation at the dinner table. They all agreed that the week had been a success, but Brother had a question.

"Mama," he asked, "what is it you don't like about TV? What do you have against it?"

"Goodness," said Mama. "I don't have anything against TV. I like it. What I'm against is the *TV habit*—sitting in front of it day after day like old stumps waiting for dry rot to set in."

"Well," said Brother, "tomorrow I'm going to get a whole bunch of snacks and watch TV all day!"

"Me, too!" said Sister.

"Me, too!" said Papa.

But the only one who did watch it all day was Papa.
Brother got interested in his cube puzzle and finally
solved it. Sister started knitting a rug on her knitting
spool.

Finally even Papa had enough, and decided to bait
his hook for a couple of those leaping trout.